DISNEY'S
THE
LION KING

1

Far away in the Pridelands, all the
animals gathered to meet Simba,
the **newborn** son of King Mufasa
and Queen Sarabi. One day, Simba
would be king.

Simba's uncle, Scar, stayed away from the celebration. "Grrr! I should be king, not Simba!"

As Simba grew, Mufasa taught him what it meant to be king. "You must learn to be a leader, Simba," Mufasa said. "One day, you will take my place as king in the great Circle of Life."

Game

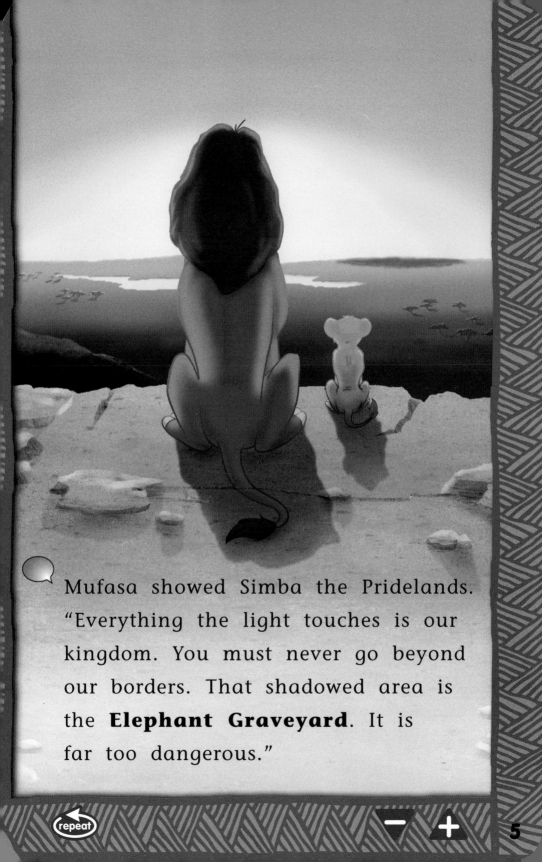

Mufasa showed Simba the Pridelands. "Everything the light touches is our kingdom. You must never go beyond our borders. That shadowed area is the **Elephant Graveyard**. It is far too dangerous."

gazelle

ostrich

zebra

elephant

baboon

meerkat

GO

One day, against his father's wishes, Simba dared his best friend, Nala, to visit the Elephant Graveyard. "Are you brave enough to come with me?"

STOP

Game 1   Game 2

As the **cubs** headed off, Mufasa's helper, Zazu, tried to keep an eye on them. Simba and Nala did their best to lose him.

GO

The Elephant Graveyard was dark and scary. Soon, the cubs were surrounded by a circle of strange creatures. **Hyenas**!

STOP

Game

Luckily, Zazu found the little lions and he rushed to tell the king! Mufasa saved Simba and Nala and returned them safely to the Pridelands.

GO

That night, Mufasa was upset. "Simba, I'm very disappointed in you. You **disobeyed** me."
"I'm sorry, Dad. I was just trying to be brave like you," Simba said.

STOP

Game 1   Game 2

"Look at the stars," said Mufasa. "The great kings of the past look down on us from those stars. They will always be here to guide you, and so will I."

GO

Meanwhile, Scar was up to no good. The next day, he lured Simba into a canyon. "Wait here, Simba. Your father has a surprise for you," Scar lied.

Game

It was a trick! Scar sent a group of hyenas to scare the wildebeests. The wildebeests began to run wildly. Simba found himself trapped in a **stampede**!

GO

STOP

Mufasa heard the thunder of **hooves**, and he ran to the rescue. He saved Simba, but he could not save himself. The great king died.

Game

"Simba, what have you done? Run away and never return!" Scar said. Heartbroken, Simba left the Pridelands and headed toward the jungle.

Sad and alone in the **jungle**, Simba met two new friends, Timon and Pumbaa. They helped cheer him up.

"You've got to put your past behind you, kid," said Timon. "Repeat after me: Hakuna Matata! It means 'no worries'."

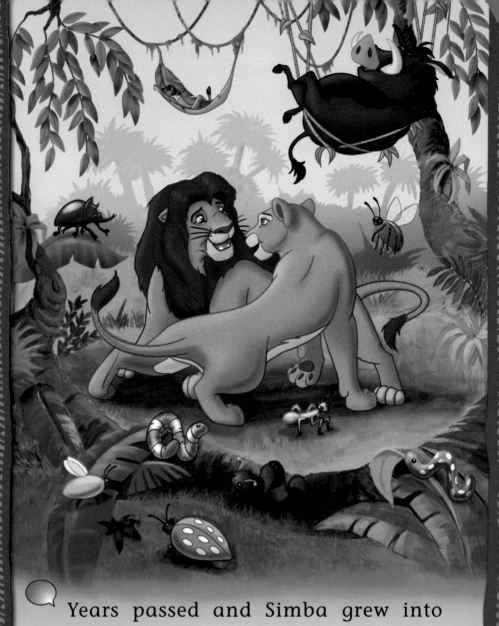

Years passed and Simba grew into a strong lion. One day, his old friend, Nala, **wandered** into the jungle in search of food. "Simba, you're alive!" she cried.

GO

STOP

18

Game

"You have to come back to the Pridelands! Scar has let the hyenas take over the kingdom. Everything is destroyed. There is no food or water. You're our only hope!"

Simba was **confused**. That night, Mufasa spoke to him from the stars above. "Remember who you are, Simba. You are my son, and the one true king."

Simba knew what he had
to do. He returned to the
Pridelands. "This is my kingdom,
Scar! Step down!" Scar lunged for
Simba, but he was no match for
the young lion.

Simba was king at last.
High **atop** Pride Rock, he and
his queen, Nala, rejoiced at the
birth of their new cub. The Circle
of Life continued.

Game

repeat

The End

Did you enjoy that story?

Check out these sample pages from *Alphabet Adventures,* Lesson 1 in the LeapPad Phonics Program and *Lots and Lots of Honeypots,* a fantastic LeapStart math book!

Let's Meet the Alphabet!

Aa
apple

Bb
bat

Cc
cat

Gg
gorilla

Hh
hat

I i
igloo

Mm
moon

Nn
net

Oo
octopus

Ss
sun

Tt
tent

Uu
umbrella

Yy
yo-yo

SAY IT

SOUND IT

C-A-T!
SPELL IT

Dd
d o g

Ee
elephant

Ff
f o x

 GO

Jj
j e t

Kk
k i t e

Ll
l i z a r d

Pp
p i g

Qq
q u e e n

Rr
r a b b i t

Vv
v a n

Ww
w a g o n

Xx
x - r a y

Zz
z e b r a

A a

arm

ant

apple

Amazing A
announces the ABCs.

B b

GO

ball

box

bear

bat

💬 Big B blows bubbles.

One day Pooh saw his little friend Piglet pulling a wagon. "What's in your wagon?" asked Pooh.

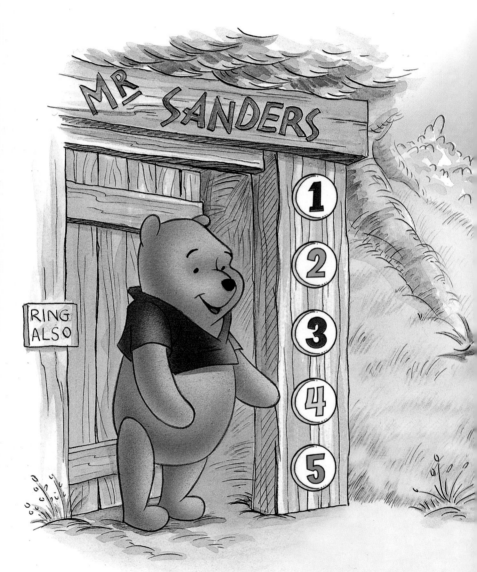

NUMBERS GAME

COUNTING GAME

repeat

Keep your child learning by leaps and bounds with the Never-Ending Learning™ Club!

Activity Sheets Available Online!

Fun activities like those found in your LeapPad® Learning System books are also available online in a convenient 12-month subscription. With a Mind Station™ connector, you can print Activity Sheets right at home on your own printer! Yearly subscriptions are available for **Kindergarten & 1st Grade.**

Leap's Pond™ Interactive Magazine

Thrill your child with *Leap's Pond* magazine packed with puzzles, games, stories and activities. Use the Mind Station connector and reusable cartridge to download the dazzling interactive content that makes the magic of *Leap's Pond* magazine come to life. You'll find selections from 6 core curriculum areas in each issue. *Ages 4-7.*

The *Mind Station™* connector works with LeapFrog.com to transfer fun and challenging activities to a reusable cartridge. Pop the cartridge in your LeapPad player and bring materials to life!

Purchase a *Mind Station™* connector and join the Never-Ending Learning Club. You'll have access to new activities for all of your Internet-enabled LeapFrog and Quantum Leap® learning toys.*

* A computer and Internet connection are required

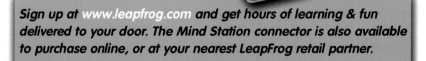